SECOND CHANCE
RANCH

LLAMA DRAMA

A GRACE STORY

Book design by Jake Nordby
Illustrations by Jomike Tejido

Published in the United States by Jolly Fish Press, an imprint of North Star Editions, Inc.

First Edition
First Printing, 2018

This is a work of fiction. Names, characters, places, and incidents are either the product of the author's imagination or are used fictitiously, and any resemblance to actual persons living or dead, business establishments, events, or locales is entirely coincidental.

Library of Congress Cataloging-in-Publication Data
Names: Abrams, Kelsey, author. | Tejido, Jomike, illustrator.
Title: Llama drama : a Grace story / Kelsey Abrams ; illustrated by Jomike Tejido. Description: Mendota Heights, MN : Jolly Fish Press, [2019] | Series: Second Chance Ranch | Summary: "Grace attempts to train Harry, a llama, as part of her science project"—Provided by publisher.
Identifiers: LCCN 2018032139 (print) | LCCN 2018039489 (ebook) | ISBN 9781631632655 (e-book) | ISBN 9781631632648 (pbk.) | ISBN 9781631632631 (hardcover)
Subjects: | CYAC: Llamas—Training—Fiction. | Science projects—Fiction. | Sisters—Fiction. | Animal rescue Fiction. | Schools—Fiction. | Family life—Fiction. | Ranch life—Fiction. | Hispanic Americans—Fiction.
Classification: LCC PZ7.1.A18 (ebook) | LCC PZ7.1.A18 Ll 2019 (print) | DDC [Fic]—dc23
LC record available at https://lccn.loc.gov/2018032139

Jolly Fish Press
North Star Editions, Inc.
2297 Waters Drive
Mendota Heights, MN 55120
www.jollyfishpress.com

Printed in the United States of America

LLAMA DRAMA

A GRACE STORY

KELSEY ABRAMS

ILLUSTRATED BY JOMIKE TEJIDO

TEXT BY LAURIE J. EDWARDS

JOLLY FiSH PRESS
Mendota Heights, Minnesota

Chapter One

Grace fanned herself with her hand. The dry, dusty air blowing in the SUV windows did little to cool the broiling afternoon heat. The temperature seemed more like midsummer than springtime. "Hey, Mom, can we stop for an ice cream cone?"

"Sounds good to me," her twin sister, Emily, said.

Mrs. Ramirez blew out a loud breath. "Unfortunately, these errands can't take all afternoon. I need to get back to the clinic later today. I have a group of students from the veterinary program at the state college coming for a tour at 3:30."

"But your vet office is supposed to be closed on Saturday afternoons," Grace complained.

"It normally is, but I thought it would be easier to talk to the students and show them around when I wasn't busy with appointments. I'm sorry, sweetie."

Natalie, who was usually the peacemaker in the family, suggested, "Maybe you could drop them at the petting zoo just outside of town and pick them up on the way home. They could get ice cream there, and it would give them something to do while they wait."

"I don't know," Mrs. Ramirez said. "If we're looking for new boots for you and then doing grocery shopping, they'd be there for two hours."

"Please, Mom," Grace begged. "I love the petting zoo. We don't mind being there for a long time, do we, Emily?"

"No, we don't. It would be fun," Emily said.

"Look at it this way, Mom," Natalie said, "we can get done faster if it's just the two of us. You know how Grace fusses after we've been shopping for a while."

"Hey!" Grace crossed her arms and glared at Natalie.

Her twelve-year-old sister winked at her and mimed zipping her mouth shut. *I'm trying to convince Mom*, she mouthed.

Mrs. Ramirez sighed. "It would be easier, but I worry about them."

"We're nine years old, Mom," Grace said. "Not babies."

"Nine-year-olds can still get into trouble."

"We'll behave," Emily promised. "And you know you can count on Abby to be good."

Their ten-year-old sister, Abby, smiled at Emily. "I'd like ice cream, and I really want to observe some of the animals. I've been reading about peacocks, and the petting zoo has two."

Mrs. Ramirez laughed. "Peacocks aren't exactly animals you can pet."

"You can't pet all the animals," Abby explained. "Some of them you just have to look at or feed, like the ducks and turkeys."

"I suppose if the three of you stay together and promise not to get into any trouble"—Mrs. Ramirez directed a pointed look at Grace in the rearview mirror—"I guess it will be okay."

Grace thrust out her lower lip. *That's not fair! How come Mom singled me out with that look?* She almost said it aloud, but as Mrs. Ramirez flipped on her left turn signal and waited for an opportunity to cross the traffic, Grace forgot about her irritation. They were turning onto the road to the petting zoo! *Ice cream and animals instead of shopping and errands. What could be better?*

"Yay!" Grace shouted when they pulled into the parking lot.

Mrs. Ramirez jumped at the sound, and Abby covered her ears, but Grace was so happy, she didn't care. She hopped out of the car and started to take off, but her mom's sharp "Grace!" made her turn and trudge back to the car. She disliked lectures, but from the look on her mom's face, she was about to get one.

Mrs. Ramirez pulled out some bills and handed them to Abby. "That should be enough for ice cream, entrance fees to the petting zoo, and some animal feed."

Grace was bouncing up and down on her toes, eager to get moving, but her mom beckoned for her to come closer. Sighing, Grace complied and tried to stop jiggling.

"Okay, you three," Mrs. Ramirez said, with a serious look on her face, "I meant what I said about staying together. That means you, Grace."

Grace crossed her arms. "Why just me?"

"Because when you get excited, you often rush into things. Try to slow your pace to Emily's and Abby's. You'll have plenty of time to see everything." Mrs. Ramirez glanced at her watch. "We should be back around 2:30, so keep an eye on the time."

All three girls nodded. Then they stuck together as they headed for the entrance.

"Thanks, Mom!" Emily called over her shoulder, and the other girls added their thanks.

"I'm really hot," Grace said. "Can we get our ice cream first?"

"Fine with me." Abby headed for the creamery beside the entrance gate.

After they chose their flavors and paid for their cones, Emily suggested staying inside the air-conditioned building until they cooled off. Grace finished her cone first and swung her legs impatiently, waiting for the other two to finish. Finally, they were done, and they headed out the door.

Abby paid their entrance fees, and Grace stayed close to her sisters as they went through the revolving turnstile.

"Where should we go first?" Grace asked.

"Why don't we start at the pond?" Abby suggested.

"Then we could do the inner loop and end up at the outer loop by the time Mom comes back."

Grace had hoped to see the peacocks first, but Abby's plan made sense, so she held back her protest and walked with her sisters toward the tiny pond. Abby stopped to buy duck food from the vending machines. With their hands full, the sisters approached the railing around the pond. Ducks, geese, and swans swam toward them, eager to be fed.

"Wow, look at that swan. I think they're the most beautiful birds," Emily said. "I wish I had my camera and sketchbook."

"I think peacocks are prettier," Grace said. "You have your phone, don't you? You could use that to take pictures."

Emily felt around in her pockets and pulled out her phone. "Can you hold my duck food while I snap a few pictures?" She dumped the feed into Abby's outstretched hand. Then she took several pictures of the various birds.

Grace tossed her feed into the water, and the birds fought over it. When her hand was empty, she was ready to move on. She wanted to head toward the nearby hill where they housed the peacocks, but remembering her mother's warning, she stayed where she was while Emily took photo after photo. Grace sighed loudly to signal that she wanted to go.

"Just a few more, Grace, I promise." Emily rested

her elbows on the railing and kept tapping the button. "Let's take a selfie with the birds in the background."

The three sisters huddled together, one on each side of Emily, as she snapped a picture. "Lean back more against the rail," she said, "so I can get the swan in the background. Okay, smile."

"Girls!" a man's voice barked nearby. "Could you move out of the way, please?"

Startled, they all jumped, and Emily almost

dropped her phone. They stepped away from the railing as the end of a huge net came sailing toward them.

A short, bald man in hip-high wading boots shoved behind them. "Move, please," he said sharply as he reached for the flying net. He caught it and draped it over the railing.

The sisters had moved back far enough to observe him. He tacked the edges down with plastic stakes he'd pulled from his pocket. Then he motioned to someone on the other side of the small artificial lake and pointed to his right.

"You go over there!" he yelled. "I'll take this side."

When he walked past them, Grace asked, "What are you doing?"

"Trapping the birds." The man walked briskly to the side he'd indicated and tacked the netting down.

"Did he say they're trapping birds?" Grace's voice was shrill.

Emily had a worried frown on her face. "That's what it sounded like."

"Hey!" Grace charged after the man. "Why are you trapping the birds?"

"Because I bought them," he snapped.

Grace stood there, confused, as her sisters came running over. "You can't do that," she told him. "These birds belong to the petting zoo."

"Not for long." The man bent to drive in the final stake. He tapped it down with his foot.

His words worried Grace. "What's that supposed to mean?" she asked.

"If you don't pay your bills, you lose your property." The bald man started to walk the perimeter, bending to check the stakes, and Grace trailed after him.

"Lose your property?" she repeated. "Are you taking all the animals?"

The man shook his head. "No, only the birds."

"Come on, Grace!" Emily called. "Let's go look at the inner loop of animals."

But Grace was upset and wanted to find out more about the birds. She kept following the man; he rounded the end of the small lake and met the other worker.

"All secure, Bert?" he asked. When Bert nodded, the bald man said, "They can't fly far with this netting in place, so we should be able to capture them easily. Go get the cages and feed, and let's get this taken care of." He donned long, thick leather gloves, undid a stake, slipped under the netting, and replaced the stake.

The netting hung so low, he had to hunch over to walk.

Bert returned, lugging several cages, and also lifted up the netting to slip underneath, replacing the stakes when he was in position. He was even taller than the bald man, so he knelt near the edge of the pond and ducked his head.

Bert lifted a cage and propped open the door. He had on the same long, thick gloves. "Ready when you are," he said. "You want me to toss a little food on the ground now, Mr. Harris?"

"Let me wade in and see how many I can catch first before we use food."

Mr. Harris strode into the water, and birds flew up, only to hit the netting. They flapped their wings, squawked, and whirled in panicked circles. He dove toward one duck, who pecked at him and then took off. He pivoted and lunged for another.

Abby and Emily caught up with Grace. Emily sucked in a breath. "He's frightening those birds. How can he be so mean?"

"I think he's just trying to catch them," Abby said.

"All he has to do is stand there. They'll come over to him if he's quiet enough," Emily insisted.

"That's easy for you to say, Emily," Grace said. "You're an animal whisperer. If you stand there, they'll come. I don't think they'd come to this guy."

"You may be right." Emily winced as Mr. Harris grabbed a goose, waded to the shore, and shoved it in a cage.

Just then, the owner of the petting zoo, Mr. Williams, strode over. A cheerful man with a white beard, he was a familiar sight at the zoo. He loved walking around and talking to visitors. The girls had met him many times. Today, though, rather than his usual smile, his shoulders slumped, and he had a glum expression.

Grace dashed over to him. "Mr. Williams," she said, "why are those men taking the birds? They said you didn't pay your bills. Is that true?"

Mr. Williams's? lips twisted into a grimace. "No, Grace—it is Grace, isn't it?"

Grace's ponytail bobbed up and down as she nodded. "Oh, good," she said. "I was worried about you. I thought we could have a fundraiser like my soccer team does to raise money."

"That's sweet of you." He smiled, but it didn't reach his eyes. "I have enough money, but the township is making me close down the zoo due to zoning regulations. I need to get rid of all the animals within the next two weeks."

"*All* of them?" Grace screeched. "We love the petting zoo. I'm going to miss this place!"

"I hope you'll still stop by for ice cream." He turned as Mr. Harris and Bert slipped outside the netting and headed toward him. "Excuse me a minute. I need to talk to these men."

Mr. Harris hurried over. "Look, I know that we said we'd pay for these birds, but now that I've seen them up close, I don't think they're worth half of that. Their meat will be awfully tough."

Mr. Williams paled. "Meat? I thought you said you had a duck farm."

"We do. We process meat for a major food processor."

"Meat?!" Grace was appalled. "The ducks and geese aren't going to be eaten, are they?"

Pinching his lips together, Mr. Williams rocked back on his heels. "Well . . ."

Mr. Harris said, "Yes, they are, as long as we can come to an agreement on price."

Grace stomped her foot. "No, you can't kill them. We won't let you." She nudged Emily, who'd come to stand beside her. "Tell him he can't do it, Em."

Her sister stopped sniffling and added her plea to Grace's. "Please don't hurt them."

"When I made this arrangement," Mr. Williams said, "I didn't know what you had in mind. I didn't think you had plans to kill them for meat." He pulled a handkerchief out of his pocket, turned his back, and honked into it a few times before turning to face them. "I'm not sure what to do. If I turned them out into the wild, they wouldn't survive. That would be even crueler."

"So why not give them to someone who would care for them?" Grace asked.

"I tried, but I haven't had much luck. And I'm still figuring out what to do with the other animals.

They're not exotic enough for zoos, but many of them are too unusual for pets."

Grace couldn't let any of these petting zoo animals get hurt. "We'll take them. All of the animals."

"Um, Grace," Emily said, "you need to ask Mom and Dad first."

Mr. Williams laughed. "I'm sure plenty of kids would love to take all the animals home, but I suspect when you ask your parents, they'll have a different idea."

"You don't understand," Grace told him. "My family owns Second Chance Ranch."

"The animal rehab place outside of town? Yes, I knew that, but—"

Grace interrupted, "So we're used to taking care of animals."

"I thought you cared for hurt and abused animals."

Abby answered him. "We do, but we take in home-less animals too." Then she turned to Grace. "I don't think we'd have enough room for all these animals at the ranch. Some of them need lots of room to roam around."

Grace wasn't about to give up without a fight. "We'll just have to make room."

Mr. Williams patted her shoulder. "I appreciate the offer, but I think your sister's right. We have too many animals."

Grace thrust out her jaw. "I'm not letting any of these animals get eaten."

"Neither am I." Mr. Williams turned to Mr. Harris. "I'm sorry I misunderstood your intent, but I don't want my birds to go to a processing plant."

Mr. Harris shrugged. "Those birds would be too old and tough. I am going to charge you for our work time, though. And we still have to remove the netting."

"Fair enough." Mr. Williams pulled out his wallet. "How much do I owe you?" After Mr. Harris named a number, Mr. Williams counted out bills and handed them over.

Bert and Mr. Harris walked to the duck pond and began disassembling the netting they'd staked down. Then Bert opened the cages, and the ducks waddled to the pond.

Grace smiled. "I'm so glad they're not turning them into food."

"Me too," Mr. Williams agreed, but then sighed loudly. "But now I have even more animals to find homes for."

"I already told you, we can take them to our ranch," Grace insisted.

Emily, Abby, and Mr. Williams all shook their heads.

"I don't think so," Emily leaned over to whisper.

But Grace was determined to take care of every single one of these animals.

Chapter Two

As the three girls strolled around the petting zoo, Emily remarked, "It's so sad to think about this petting zoo closing. I love coming here. I guess I should take as many pictures as I can while we're here."

"You can take as many as you want soon," Grace assured her. "Mom and Dad won't turn away needy animals."

Emily only shook her head.

Abby led them to the peacocks. "I've been reading about peacocks. Did you know only the males are called *peacocks*? The females are called *peahens*. Babies are *peachicks*." She studied the two birds roaming the hill. "The zoo labeled them correctly. They're both males."

"How can you tell?" Grace studied the birds' beautiful iridescent trailing tails. She wished they'd fan out their tails to show their blue-and-green feathers with the eye-shaped design on them.

"Only the males have brilliantly colored tails, so these must both be males." Abby propped her elbows on the top of the fencing and studied the two birds.

"Their tails are so long," Emily said as the peacocks strutted along, dragging their tails along behind them.

"They're usually about six feet long," Abby said. She pointed to the one closest to them. "This one looks like it might be even longer than that. I wish I could measure it to see."

All of a sudden, that peacock fanned out his tail, and Grace sucked in a breath. Sunshine shimmered on its feathers, making them look like tiny crystals. "It's so beautiful," she said softly.

"I wish I could hear its feathers," Abby said as the bird's feathers vibrated.

"We did," Grace pointed out. "They made a swishing sound."

"I heard that," Abby said, "but their feathers quiver and make a low-frequency sound that people

can't hear. They shake different parts of their feathers to change the sound to signal females to come closer."

"Really?" Grace leaned partway over the fence, trying to hear the sound, but she couldn't. She sighed. "I wish I could hear it too."

Emily, who was busy snapping pictures, added, "That would be so awesome to hear."

After they finished, the girls moved on. Grace hurried them along until they reached the llama. The last time they'd been here, there'd been two llamas in the enclosure. Today, only one stuck his head over the fencing.

"Stay back," Emily warned. "You know how they spit."

"It's not spit," Abby reminded her. She'd told them several times before when they visited the zoo. "It's actually throw up."

"Eww," Grace said, but she ignored her sister's warning and moved close enough to reach a hand through the mesh and stroke the llama's coat, but the llama turned its back and walked away. "Aww, I wanted to pet you."

"Llamas are one of my favorites," Emily said. "I wish he'd turn around so I could get some pictures."

"They're my favorites too," Grace said. She huffed out a breath. "I wish he'd let me pet him."

"It doesn't look like he's going to come over here,"

Abby said, "so why don't we go look at some other animals?"

They moved on to other enclosures, where they could pet some of the animals. Emily took pictures of most of them. Then she glanced at her phone. "It's almost 2:30. We should probably go out to meet Mom."

They skipped looking at the last few animals and hurried through the turnstile to sit at one of the picnic tables in front of the creamery. Grace drummed her fingers on the table. She wished her mom would hurry. She couldn't wait to ask her about taking the animals. They'd have to expand their enclosures, but their ranch was large enough to do that. It would be a big job, but they'd often helped their dad repair fencing. If they all pitched in . . .

She spied their SUV turning in and jumped to her feet. Mr. Williams must have seen it, too, because he appeared in the entrance of the petting zoo.

"I'd like to talk to your mom, girls!" he called as he headed down the sidewalk toward them.

When Mrs. Ramirez pulled into a parking space, Grace was waiting on the sidewalk nearby, dancing from one foot to the other. She glanced around to be sure no cars were coming before dashing to her mom's car. "Mom, Mom, we have to take care of the animals here," she said through the open window. "They don't have any place to go, and the ducks almost got sold to a man who was going to turn them into food."

Mrs. Ramirez shot her a questioning glance, but by then, Emily and Abby had reached the car and were standing next to Grace. Mr. Williams hesitated on the sidewalk nearby, as if unsure whether to approach the vehicle.

"Mom, the petting zoo is closing," Abby informed her. "Mr. Williams has problems with zoning, so all the animals need homes."

"Oh, no, that's sad. From time to time, he brings one of his animals to my clinic. He seems to really love them."

"He does," Grace said. "That's why I told him we'd take all his animals."

Mrs. Ramirez laughed nervously. "I hope he realized you were joking."

"Joking?" Grace stamped her foot. "I wasn't joking. I was serious."

"Honey, we can't possibly take that many animals. Where in the world would we put them?"

"We have lots of land. We could build some extra pens and—"

"What about feeding them?" her mom asked. "Do you have any idea how much that would cost?"

Mr. Williams crossed the parking lot. "Hi, Mrs. Ramirez." He set a hand on Grace's shoulder. "You have a generous and thoughtful daughter here."

"Yes, Grace does have a good heart." Mrs. Ramirez

tapped her fingers on the steering wheel. "I, um, hope she didn't give you the wrong impression."

"The thing is," Mr. Williams said, "I didn't realize your ranch also took in homeless animals. I just assumed with you being a vet and all, well, they'd be animals needing medical care or something."

"Some animals do come to us needing special care, but we also take in abandoned animals. However . . ." Mrs. Ramirez cleared her throat.

Mr. Williams held up a hand. "I understand, believe me. I did tell your daughter I have too many animals to send them all to you, but I wondered, if I find homes for most of them, if you'd be willing to take the ones that are left."

"I suppose—" Mrs. Ramirez started to say, but Grace interrupted.

"Of course we will. You have to say *yes*, Mom."

"I'd be happy to pay for their care," Mr. Williams said. "But if you don't feel you can take on additional animals right now, I completely understand."

"Why don't I discuss it with my husband and have a family meeting about it?" Mrs. Ramirez told him. "The girls are the ones who will end up with many of the extra daily chores of feeding and cleaning, so they should have some input in the decision."

"Certainly, certainly. I understand. I appreciate you even considering it, and if you have any ideas of places that might take some of the animals, I'd be open to whatever tips you might have."

"I'll ask around at the office to see, and I'll let you know about taking the other animals."

That night at dinner, Grace wriggled in her chair until family sharing time, then she burst out with her news, "The petting zoo is closing, and I told Mr. Williams we'd take his animals."

Mr. Ramirez's eyebrows rose. "Not all of them, I hope." He chuckled, but when no one else did, his laughter died. He turned to his wife with a question in his eyes. At Mrs. Ramirez's tight smile, he said, "All right, what's going on?"

Mrs. Ramirez took a deep breath. "I thought we could have a family meeting tonight to discuss the situation. Evidently, Mr. Williams has run into a zoning problem and has two weeks to get rid of all of his animals. He's having trouble finding homes for them. Grace kindly offered to take all of them."

"And you explained why we couldn't do that?" he asked with an anxious look on his face.

"Of course, but Mr. Williams wondered if we could house the leftover animals," she told her husband.

He blew out a breath. "I guess that's better than

taking all of them, but still . . . Do you have any idea how many that would be?"

"I have no idea," she admitted, "but he did offer to pay for their keep."

"That would be a help, of course, but how many animals can we take when we're already close to capacity?" He rubbed his forehead.

"That's what I'd hoped to discuss tonight, as well as who'd be caring for the animals. But why don't we save this discussion for after dinner?" Mrs. Ramirez nodded in Grace's direction. "Did you have anything more you wanted to share?"

After Grace told about the men trying to trap the birds under the netting, Abby shared about peacocks. Then Emily talked about some of the animals she photographed and their funny poses. Natalie told about her new boots, and Mrs. Ramirez discussed the college tour.

"In fact," she said, "several local students asked about being interns at the clinic over the summer. It would be great to have some extra help."

"It certainly would," Mr. Ramirez agreed. "You work much too hard. And it would be a learning experience for the students to assist in the clinic."

"Maybe some of the interns would like to help at the ranch," Grace suggested.

"Hmm . . ." Mrs. Ramirez stared thoughtfully into the distance. "That might be a possibility. They also might know of people who would take in some of the animals."

"Brilliant." Mr. Ramirez smiled at her. Then he launched into a tale about transporting two pigs to a family on a nearby ranch. "Thanks to your website, Natalie, we placed two more animals today, although," he said, his expression rueful, "it looks like we freed up two spaces when we're going to need a whole bunch."

Following the meal, they gathered in the family room to discuss the petting zoo situation.

"So first we need to find out how many animals the zoo has right now," Mr. Ramirez said.

Mrs. Ramirez nodded. "And I suppose we should also find out what he's done about placing them."

"Maybe we could help him," Natalie suggested. "I could put a section on the website showing the animals he has."

"What a wonderful idea," Mrs. Ramirez said. "We have a lot of visitors to our site who are looking for animals."

"I have pictures of most of them," Emily said. "I can give you those. Maybe we could go back tomorrow and get pictures of the rest."

Mr. Ramirez nodded. "That might be wise. Then we can hammer out some of the arrangements, find out what animals are spoken for, and make plans with Mr. Williams."

"I guess the other thing we need to figure out is who's willing to do extra chores to take care of the animals." Mrs. Ramirez glanced around the room.

Grace groaned the loudest, and Abby looked at her in surprise. "But this was your idea."

"I know, but I wasn't thinking it would mean extra chores." Grace's lips twisted, then she sighed. "I know, I know. If we take in the animals, someone has to care for them."

All three of her sisters stared at her.

Grace sat there open-mouthed. "Wait a minute, you don't mean you expect me to do all the jobs by myself?"

"Like Abby said, it was your idea," Natalie pointed out.

"But, but, but . . ." Grace's mouth opened and closed like a fish's.

Then Natalie giggled, and the others joined her. "Don't worry. We'll help."

"*Whew.*" Grace blew out a long breath. "I thought you were serious."

"I hope you realize how much extra work this might be, depending on how many animals we need to take," Mrs. Ramirez said. "I'm glad you girls are all willing to pitch in."

"I have another idea," Emily said. "I could make posters advertising the animals that we could put up in town."

"That's a great idea, Em," Grace said. "You take such nice pictures. With your posters and Natalie's website, we should be able to find more homes for the animals." Then her mouth turned down. "But I was hoping we could keep all of them."

"I know you were, honey," Mrs. Ramirez said, "but that would be way too much work. You'd be doing chores all day long."

"I wouldn't like that," Grace agreed. "And we'll be finding good homes for them. I guess that's the most important thing." Then, her eyes wide, she said, "We'll check all possible owners to be sure they're going to care for the animals properly, right?"

"Of course," Mrs. Ramirez assured her. "We'll only accept good homes."

"That's good," Grace said. "If we can't have them ourselves, I want them to have nice homes."

Chapter Three

The next afternoon, the family headed for the petting zoo to talk to Mr. Williams. He'd drawn up a list of the animals and checked off the ones he'd placed.

"I think a zoo in the city will take the kangaroo," he said, "and a family claimed the two potbellied pigs, but not the Berkshire pig or the teacup pigs. And a local farmer agreed to take the lambs, but not the two older sheep—"

Grace broke into the conversation. "He's not going to eat them, is he?"

Mr. Williams shook his head. "No, he breeds sheep, so he'll be good to them."

He listed all the smaller animals who would come with cages and equipment, including a chinchilla, two teacup pigs, two hedgehogs, several lizards, bunnies, hamsters, a ferret, guinea pigs, a descented skunk, gerbils, a tortoise, and more.

Mrs. Ramirez turned rather pale as the list went on. "And that's just the *small* animals?" she asked faintly.

"Yes, some of those will make good pets, but I haven't reached out to pet store owners or individuals yet."

"We're going to do that," Emily said shyly. "I'm making posters to hang in town."

"We can also pass out flyers at our school," Grace added.

Natalie smiled at her. "That's a great idea. I'll take some to my school too."

Mr. Williams nodded. "Why didn't I think of that? Lots of those children come here to visit the petting zoo. I expect we'd need to get permission from the principals, but if your mom or dad could email me a copy of your flyers, Emily, I'll see about getting them printed and handed out to several different area school districts."

"I could also make one that says, *Would you like to take me home?*" Emily offered. "You could hang one by each cage or enclosure."

"I should have come to you girls for ideas," Mr. Williams said, smiling. "I hadn't thought to approach visitors. I was trying to find places that would take as many as possible."

"Maybe an ad in the newspaper—letting people know you're closing and you're looking for homes for the animals—might bring in some interest," Mr. Ramirez suggested.

"I thought about that. The only thing I worry about, though, is whether the people who show up would love and care for the animals."

Mrs. Ramirez looked thoughtful. "Perhaps some

of the veterinary students might be willing to check out the people who respond. I could ask my friend who heads up the program at the college. And I think everyone who comes to my office is an animal lover. I can put up a poster there."

"Hopefully by putting out the flyers, we can find homes for most of the small animals," Mr. Williams said. "Most of them will make good pets because they're used to children touching them. The larger animals are, too, so they're pretty gentle. A few can be contrary—like the miniature donkeys and the llama—but overall, they're friendly."

"I hope nobody takes the llama," Grace told him. "I've always wanted a llama."

"That's the first time I've ever heard you say that," Mrs. Ramirez said. "I had no idea."

Grace clamped her mouth shut. She wished she hadn't said that. The llama reminded her of her birth mom and her favorite stuffed animal that had somehow gotten lost in their move from Dallas. She hadn't said anything because she didn't want to hurt her adopted parents' feelings. She bit down hard on her lower lip so it would stop quivering, and she blinked to hold back tears.

Emily flashed her a sympathetic look, and her twin's eyes looked damp.

A llama wouldn't bring their birth mom back, but it might restore some of the memories that seemed to be fading away. The longer she and Emily were on the ranch and part of their new family, the harder it was to remember the past. Grace needed to hang onto it somehow.

By the time Grace tuned back in to the conversation, Mr. Williams was listing the last of the large animals—the goats and sheep—along with the Shetland pony. She'd missed the rest of the list. She'd been around the petting zoo enough to know what those were, though.

The only animal she hoped they wouldn't have to take was the huge Berkshire pig. The way he snorted and snuffled, he made her nervous. She couldn't imagine anyone wanting him for a pet. He was one of the only animals she'd never tried to pet.

"Oh," Mr. Williams said, "I forgot to mention the birds."

"There are more?" Mrs. Ramirez sounded overwhelmed.

Mr. Williams nodded. "Sorry. Yes, I have several species of ducks, some geese and swans, a few turkeys, a guinea hen, and two peacocks."

Mrs. Ramirez blinked. "I see." She seemed at a loss for words.

"I don't suppose you'll have much luck placing most of the water birds," Mr. Ramirez said.

"True," Mr. Williams said.

"It's good we have a pond, right, Dad?" Grace pointed out. "They'll feel at home there."

"I'm not sure they'd stay in our pond, Grace." Mr. Ramirez turned to Mr. Williams. "Your pond's not enclosed. How do you keep the water birds around?"

"I've never had to worry about that. They get fed so well here, they don't try to fly away."

"It seems we have a lot to think about and take care of," Mr. Ramirez said. "We should be going, but we'll be back in touch. I'll email Emily's flyers for you to print."

As they left the office, Emily stopped her dad. "I should take some pictures of the animals I missed."

"Good idea," he responded. "Why don't the rest of you get ice cream cones while I stay with Emily? What flavor would you like them to get for you, Em? I'd like butter pecan."

After they heard Emily's order for mint chocolate chip, Mrs. Ramirez herded the other girls over to the creamery.

As they waited in the long line to order, Grace said, "I wish the kangaroo wasn't going to the city zoo. Wouldn't it be cool to say we had a kangaroo at our house? Everybody at school would want to come see it."

Mrs. Ramirez laughed. "I'm very glad it has a home. With the number of people who'd want to see it, we'd need to charge admission and open our own petting zoo."

"Oooh . . . could we do that?" Grace asked. "Then we could afford to have even more animals."

"No." Mrs. Ramirez's answer was emphatic. "We care for animals. We don't show them off." She shook her head. "Can you even imagine the traffic that would generate?"

Natalie shook her head. "We'd need a parking lot like they have here."

"I suppose we could blacktop over your soccer field in the backyard." Mrs. Ramirez shot Grace a questioning glance.

The soccer field was Grace's favorite place to spend her spare time, and her friends often joined her there. "No way," she said. "I don't want to lose my field. I practice there almost every day. And where would we play when my teammates come over?"

"Honey, that's what I'm trying to get you to think about," Mrs. Ramirez explained. "You do a wonderful job of coming up with new and creative ideas. Then you need to figure out how you'd make them work out. That's what I mean when I tell you to stop and think before you do things."

"I'm betting you wish Grace had done that before offering to take on a petting zoo, huh, Mom?" Natalie shot a teasing glance in Grace's direction.

"Actually, I do. But then again, these animals do need to be rescued, so . . ."

"Exactly." Grace put her hands on her hips. "If I hadn't told Mr. Williams we'd take the animals, what would have happened to them?"

Natalie ruffled her hair. "You're right. They did need help."

The line had inched forward while they were talking, and now it was their turn to order. Grace took Emily's cone, and Natalie took their dad's. Then they hurried over to the petting zoo.

Mr. Williams was talking to a small group of visitors near the entrance, and he let them in through his gate rather than the turnstile. "Thanks so much for everything," he said. "I can't tell you how much I appreciate your help."

"We're happy to do it," Mrs. Ramirez said. "I certainly wouldn't want to see any of these animals end up homeless."

"You have a good heart, ma'am. And your daughter does too," Mr. Williams said in a choked voice.

"Don't worry, Mr. Williams," Grace said. "We'll take very good care of your animals."

"I know you will," he responded.

Emily's ice cream dribbled down the cone and over Grace's hand. "I'd better get this to my sister." She hurried off, licking Emily's dripping ice cream. Her sister wouldn't mind if she ate a little of it, so she licked all the melty bits. And while she did, she wished she'd gotten mint chocolate chip ice cream. She liked it better than the birthday cake flavor she'd chosen. She'd picked it because it was the prettiest one, with its multicolored stripes of pink, blue, green, and yellow. Maybe this was another time she should have thought ahead.

Her dad and Emily were headed toward her. Natalie must have gotten to them much faster than Grace had, because her dad was already eating his ice cream cone. Grace rushed over to give Emily hers.

They strolled around the zoo a bit while they finished their cones. Mrs. Ramirez remarked on the size and health of the various animals, assessing whether

she'd need to treat any of them if they ended up at Second Chance Ranch. Then they all piled into the SUV to head home to do chores and eat dinner.

Later that day, at the dinner table, Mrs. Ramirez remarked, "Taking care of even half of those animals Mr. Williams told us about will be a major challenge. Getting proper care and feeding instructions for each of them will be time-consuming, and we'll also have to figure out who's going to do what jobs."

"I can take care of that," Abby said. "Once we know which ones are coming here, I'll look up the animals and get information from Mr. Williams. Then I'll make up a spreadsheet we can hang in the barn. I can even make separate ones for each of us, so we know what to do when."

"That's a lot of work," Mr. Ramirez said.

Abby's smile indicated she was up to the challenge. "I don't mind. I like figuring out things like that."

"That would be so helpful," Mrs. Ramirez said. "Thank you for offering, honey."

Natalie leaned over to reach the hot sauce. She doused her food with it. "Once Emily uploads the pictures she took, I'll get the information on the website. I finished my homework on Friday, so I can get started tonight."

"Awesome, Natalie," Grace said. "After that, I'll help Emily with posters."

"I guess the best thing to do is to put our ranch web address on the posters," Natalie told them. "Actually, I'll create a separate page for the zoo animals and give you that link. That way, people can tell what's still available. And I'll keep the site updated by taking off the pictures as each animal gets adopted."

"And I'll keep my fingers crossed that the animal pictures disappear quickly—or even altogether," Mrs. Ramirez said.

"*Moooommm . . .*" Grace glared at her mother. "I want some of the animals to come here."

"I'm just teasing, Grace." But she muttered under her breath, "I think."

By bedtime, Emily had created several posters and a special flyer with a list of animals that Abby had typed up from memory. The others had helped print information on them. While Mr. Ramirez emailed the flyer to Mr. Williams, Grace and Emily cleaned up the poster materials. Meanwhile, Natalie had created a new page and added all the pictures, plus descriptions Abby suggested.

"I just hope this works," Mrs. Ramirez said as they headed upstairs.

"Me too," said Grace, but secretly she was hoping only some of the animals would get adopted. And that nobody would pick the llama.

Chapter Four

After school the next day, Mr. Ramirez drove Grace and Emily into town, and they placed the posters on grocery store and laundromat bulletin boards. They asked store and restaurant owners if they could place the posters in the windows. Soon, they had posters in many places along all the main streets of town. Then they targeted some businesses farther out on the highway in both directions.

On the way home, they stopped in at the petting zoo to hang posters there and in the creamery. Mr. Williams thanked them and told them he'd gotten permission from several schools to send flyers home with the children. He hoped it would help.

By the time they got home, Natalie was already swamped with requests. "What should I do when we have more than one person asking for the same animal?"

"Start with the one who replied first," Mr. Ramirez said. "That's the fairest way to do it, but I hope your mom will have gotten some volunteers to check out the requests."

"I know some of these people," Natalie said. "And you and Mom might know others. We can start with those. Lots of people want guinea pigs and hamsters."

WOULD YOU LIKE TO TAKE ME HOME?

Contact Second Chance Ranch for more information

Before dinnertime, they'd matched three animals with homes. When Mrs. Ramirez arrived, she said four students had offered to help, and one of them wanted the chinchilla for a pet.

During their family sharing time at the table, Grace and Emily told about hanging the posters. And both of their parents cheered when Natalie said they'd placed three zoo animals and two Second Chance Ranch dogs.

"I'll email Mr. Williams tonight and arrange my schedule tomorrow so I can deliver all the animals, unless he can do it," Mr. Ramirez said. "I guess we should have made arrangements for that."

"You have so many other jobs to take care of here at the ranch," Mrs. Ramirez said. "I'm sure Mr. Williams can figure out how to get the animals to their new homes."

"Can't the people who are adopting them pick them up at the petting zoo?" Grace asked. "Then nobody would have to worry about deliveries."

"Good idea, Grace," Natalie said. "After dinner, I'll add that information to the website so people know."

🐾

Over the next week, the Ramirez family helped place fifteen animals. Grace was overjoyed that the llama's picture was still online. Every day when she came home from school, she kept her fingers crossed it would be there.

On the weekend, Tie the Knot, a wedding reception business, took the pair of swans for their lake. Two of Grace and Emily's classmates claimed the hedgehog and the ferret. A young boy took all the lizards, and an elderly man came to collect the tortoise.

The number of animals was dwindling, but they still had quite a few more to go and only five more days. Each day, as Mrs. Ramirez checked in with Natalie, her voice grew more nervous. Two clinic customers agreed to take the sheep and goats. By the time Friday arrived, everyone rushed to the computer to see what animals were left.

Grace cheered to see the llama's picture still posted on the website. Her parents weren't quite as overjoyed as she was. They also still had a skunk, a hedgehog, two miniature donkeys, two peacocks, a guinea hen, plus the turkeys, ducks, and geese. And the five-hundred-pound black pig.

"At least most of them are small," Mr. Ramirez said while fixing dinner, trying to cheer up his wife, but he wasn't quite successful. He layered the tortillas on a plate and carried the bowls of filling ingredients and condiments to the table so everyone could make their own tacos.

Mrs. Ramirez had come home from work exhausted after wrestling with several unruly animal patients. "All I wanted to do tomorrow after work was relax in a comfy chair and read a book, maybe take a nap. Instead, we'll be carting truckloads of animals and feed." She sighed as she layered spicy chicken, lettuce, salsa, and shredded cheese on her tortilla.

"But look at all the animals we found homes for in the past two weeks," Natalie pointed out. "Maybe we'll see the same amount of action this week."

"I hope so," Mrs. Ramirez replied. "I don't think

we have much hope of getting rid of the ducks and geese."

"I'm glad we're getting the peacocks," Abby said. "I've been reading all about them. And now that I know what animals we'll be getting tomorrow, I'll work up that spreadsheet."

"Great!" Mr. Ramirez smiled at her. "We'll also need the work schedule by Sunday morning, so we know who's supposed to take care of which animals."

"I'm going to pick the llama," Grace said. She added spicy ingredients to her tortilla until it was hot enough to burn the inside of her mouth, which was just the way she liked it.

Beside her, Emily added plain shredded chicken, lettuce, and cheese to hers.

"Sure you don't want something else on yours?" Grace pointed to the spices, the salsa, the jalapeño peppers, and the sauces.

Emily shook her head. "I like mine this way."

Grace couldn't even imagine eating something that bland. She and Natalie always added spice to their foods. "Ugh, that has to be tasteless."

"Not to me, it isn't." Emily was a supertaster, so all food had a stronger taste to her than to most people.

"So, what animals do you want to care for?" Grace asked her.

"The hedgehog and the skunk."

Leave it to Emily to pick the oddest animals, Grace thought.

Natalie looked around the table. "I'll take the donkeys because those are most like horses. If Abby takes the peacocks, we all have two animals so far, except for Grace. She should pick another one before we go around again."

Grace definitely didn't want the pig. And all the other animals were in groups except the guinea hen, so she chose that.

The next round, Emily selected the geese, Abby took the turkeys, and Natalie decided on the ducks.

"Hey, no fair. I got stuck with the pig." Grace felt like crying. *Why did I have to end up with the one animal I didn't want?*

Natalie started to say she'd switch, but Mrs. Ramirez interrupted her. "I think it would be good for Grace to care for the pig. This was her idea, after all, so it will be a good learning experience."

Why does everyone always think I need to learn a lesson? So what if I sometimes jump into things? I get things done, don't I? If it weren't for me, these animals wouldn't have any homes. And the ducks and geese would be sitting in someone's cooking pot.

Chapter Five

Because Mrs. Ramirez worked a half day on Saturday, they waited for her to get home before they made the first trip to the petting zoo. Mr. Ramirez had hooked up the horse trailer, and they each took a vehicle. Grace rode with her dad, hoping she could convince him to load the llama in the horse trailer first. She couldn't help jiggling on the seat; she was just so excited.

"My goodness, Grace," Mr. Ramirez said, "if it weren't for that seatbelt, I think you'd be bouncing to the ceiling. You're really happy about getting these animals, aren't you?"

"Definitely. Especially the llama. Can we take him in the first load?"

"I think it would make more sense to get the pig first. He's the biggest and heaviest, so we'll get that taken care of while we're fresh. I don't know how cooperative he'll be. But he's one of yours too."

Grace slumped in the seat. She didn't want to be reminded that she'd ended up with the last choice. Caring for him would be icky.

"You don't seem quite as thrilled with that one. Pigs are quite intelligent, and as I'm sure Abby will tell you, they're even smarter than dogs, so they make great pets."

Who cares if a pig is smarter than a dog? A dog jumps up and barks when it greets you. If the pig did that, it'd flatten me. I doubt such a heavy animal could dance in a circle for a bit of food. And I've never heard of anyone training a pig to lie down or heel. The only things pigs seem to do is snuffle and snort and grunt.

They pulled into the parking lot a short while after Mrs. Ramirez, and she and the three other girls were already loading the small cages into the back of the SUV. Mr. Williams had caged all the birds to transport them, and it hurt Grace's heart to see them cramped into such tight spaces. They'd be happier once they were free at the pond.

Mr. Williams came over. "Which animal did you want to load first?"

"I thought we'd take the largest one," Mr. Ramirez said.

With a nod, Mr. Williams led them over to the pig pen. To their surprise, the pig walked through the open gate, up the ramp, and into the horse trailer without any prodding.

"See? I told you pigs were smart." Mr. Ramirez winked at his daughter.

"Daisy is remarkable and a fast learner," Mr. Williams assured him. "You'll enjoy her. I'm going to miss her."

They loaded some of the ducks and geese cages onto the truck bed and headed back to the ranch.

As soon as they were let out of the cage, the birds reveled in their freedom. They fluttered and dove into the water. Mrs. Ramirez fed them, hoping it would help them stay at the pond. Then the family loaded into the two cars again and returned to the petting zoo for more bird cages and the llama.

Unlike the pig, the llama balked at walking up the ramp. The minute Mr. Ramirez headed toward his enclosure, the llama turned his back, shied away, and refused to cooperate. No amount of encouragement made him move.

In the end, Emily was the one to get him to move. Instead of approaching him from the front and meeting him head-on, Emily moved alongside him. Like she had with the wild mustang, Midnight, she inched her hand toward the llama, letting him see what she was doing. Coaxing him with her quiet, gentle voice, she touched him, a touch so light and feathery, it seemed she barely grazed his fur. Yet the llama moved closer, as if he enjoyed the closeness.

Emily closed her eyes, but her lips moved, as if she were begging the llama to cooperate. Then, without warning, the llama turned, headed toward Mr. Williams, and looked to be nodding.

"You know, don't you, boy?" Mr. Williams said. "You don't want to leave this place."

After Emily led the llama up the ramp and into the trailer, Mr. Williams pulled a handkerchief from his pocket, turned away from them, and made loud honking noises into the white cloth. When he turned back around, his eyes were damp. "I'm going to miss them. All of them. We've been friends for a long time."

"I'm sorry," Emily said.

Grace's heart went out to him. How hard it would be to say goodbye to animals you loved. "You can come to visit them anytime." She hoped her words would comfort him.

"I might do that," he said in a choked voice. "I'd like to peek in on them from time to time, just to see how they're doing."

"You're always welcome," Mrs. Ramirez said. "I'm sure the animals would be glad to see you."

Mr. Ramirez placed several more cages on the seats in the truck, leaving no room for additional human passengers. So the girls all piled into the SUV with their mom to return home. Mr. Williams had tears in his eyes as the two cars pulled away. Grace waved to him until he disappeared from sight. For some reason, his sorrow made it hard for her to bubble over about having a llama of her own to care for. She kept seeing Mr. Williams's sad face.

The nearer they got to the ranch, though, the more her excitement grew. *This is going to be my llama to teach and train. To bond with. To love.*

But how can I do that when I can't get him to cooperate? Maybe Emily could teach me some of her animal-whispering skills.

Grace partially twisted around in her seat until she could see her sister. She wished she could unbuckle her seatbelt, but staying belted in was a hard-and-fast rule in their family. "What did you tell the llama to get him to walk into the truck?" Grace asked.

"I told him we were friends and that we wouldn't

hurt him," Emily said. "It felt like he wanted me to come at him sideways instead of yanking him from the front. I don't know how to explain it, but I sensed he thought we were pressuring him when we all advanced on him. Wouldn't that bother you?"

"I guess so," Grace answered, but she wasn't quite sure. If she had a circle of people around her, she'd have been happy to be the center of attention. Although she supposed she wouldn't like being told what to do.

Emily continued, "I think he probably felt overwhelmed and uncertain because he had no idea what was going on."

Grace could understand that. It would be scary if people who spoke a different language stood around chattering at you, trying to get you to do something.

"Anyway, he wanted to cooperate but didn't want to leave Mr. Williams. You could see how sad they both were."

"I know," Grace said, and a lump rose in her throat.

"I hope Mr. Williams does come to visit," Emily said. "I'd like to ask him if he has any tips for handling . . . um . . . What are you going to name the llama?"

"I've been thinking about that." She didn't want to tell her family, because they might think the name was silly, but Emily would understand. She cupped her hands around her mouth and whispered, "I want to call him Harry after the stuffed animal I had back when Mom—our birth mom, I mean—was alive."

Emily nodded. "I like it. Harry's a good name."

Grace couldn't believe her sister had said it out loud like that. Didn't she understand that Grace had whispered for a reason?

"Is that what you plan to call him?" Mrs. Ramirez asked. "That's a cute name. Harry is definitely hairy."

A lump in her throat, Grace nodded. "That's what I was thinking." *So maybe it isn't such a silly idea after all.*

She swiveled again so she could see Emily. "I wanted to say you did a good job with Harry. Thanks for getting him into the truck," Grace said before turning back around in her seat.

She was grateful Emily had helped, but in another way, she couldn't help being a little jealous that her sister could get the llama to obey when nobody else could. Grace pictured Emily snuggling the llama. *This was supposed to be* my *llama, not Emily's. What if the llama prefers Emily?*

When they got home, Emily had to lead the llama to the enclosure their dad had created. Once Harry was inside, he turned his back to Grace, the way he'd done the other day. He did it again when she went to feed him dinner. He flicked his stubby, furry tail at her.

"Why does he do that?" she asked her mom, who was nearby making sure the animals were adjusting well to their new homes.

"He might be upset that we've moved him from the only home he's ever known and deprived him of his keeper," Mrs. Ramirez said.

"But he has me to take care of him now," Grace protested. "I'll take good care of you, Harry, I promise." But the llama didn't budge.

She wanted to see Harry's face, so she unlocked the gate to the enclosure, but her mother stopped her.

"Don't go in there," Mrs. Ramirez said. "Llamas can be temperamental. Let's give him a little time to adjust. I don't know if he's dangerous."

Grace closed the gate reluctantly. "He's not dangerous. Mr. Williams wouldn't have had him in the petting zoo if he'd hurt anyone."

"Be careful when you do go in. I'm sure he's probably fine. But just because he allowed people to pet him when he was in the zoo doesn't mean he'll accept you getting close to him inside the enclosure. And Mr. Williams did say he could be contrary."

"But Emily snuggled up to him." Grace knew she sounded whiny, but she couldn't help it.

"I know, but your sister's a bit different when it comes to animals. She seems to be able to sense what they need."

Grace crossed her arms and couldn't help the way

her face twisted into a pout. She turned away so her mom couldn't see it. Her mom didn't like grumpy expressions. She'd tell her to turn her frown upside down. Right now, though, Grace wanted to stay upset.

"How come Emily can charm animals, but I can't?"

"I imagine you could too if you'd slow down a bit," her mom said. "Did you ever notice how quiet Emily gets when she's calming animals? She stands very still and spends a lot of time listening first."

Grace nibbled on her lower lip and tried to squash down the feelings of inadequacy. *Of course, Emily does everything right.* Her voice a little teary, she said, "Yeah, and I barge in without thinking and scare them."

"Oh, honey." Her mom put her arms around her daughter and hugged her. "You and Emily have very different personalities, but you each have your own strengths."

Right now, Grace was struggling to think of any strengths she had. Her lips quivering, she said, "Emily's are better."

Mrs. Ramirez shook her head, pulling back to look at her daughter. "No personality is better than another. Emily's good at listening and communicating with animals."

"And schoolwork," Grace added.

"That one is your choice," Mrs. Ramirez reminded

her. "Your strengths are your friendliness, your courage, your big heart, your willingness to help . . ."

"I guess." Grace scuffed her toe in the dust outside the enclosure. "But I'd rather have Emily's strengths."

"It might seem like it at times, but you wouldn't want to give up your true self." Mrs. Ramirez's eyes twinkled. "I'm sure there are times Emily wishes she could be you."

"I doubt it," Grace said, her voice wavering.

"Of course she does. You know how hard it is for her to speak up and to make friends." Mrs. Ramirez smiled down at Grace. "Those things seem easy for you, but many people struggle with that."

Grace found that hard to believe. Maybe strengths were just things that came easily to you. If so, it must be easy for Emily to be quiet and listen. Grace couldn't imagine that ever being easy, but perhaps it wasn't a struggle for her sister.

Mrs. Ramirez hugged Grace again. "I'm grateful that you each have your own strengths."

"And weaknesses," Grace added.

"Let's call them *growth points*," Mrs. Ramirez suggested. "Yes, everyone has areas that could use improvement."

"*You* don't."

"Of course I do. I get grumpy and irritable when I'm feeling stressed, and I tend to worry a lot. Your dad's a good balance for that because he's always so cheerful, and he tends to look on the bright side."

Maybe it's good to be around someone who's the opposite of you. Like Emily. She and her sister did help each other out a lot. They each had strengths where the other person had weaknesses—or *growth points*, as her mom called them—so they got along well.

"If they're growth points, does that mean I need to grow?" she asked her mom.

Mrs. Ramirez nodded. "That's the point. They're areas where you can improve."

Grace decided to pick two growth points to work on—getting better grades in science and trying to be more patient, to do things slowly instead of barging right in. Maybe she could practice that with Harry. She decided to keep her plans to herself, though, in case she didn't do as well as she'd like.

Chapter Six

On Monday evening at the dinner table, Emily shared about the science project their teacher, Ms. Montes, had assigned. "We have to come up with a hypothesis and design an experiment that takes several weeks to prove."

Grace couldn't believe Emily would choose the science project for her upbeat news to share. *Who considers homework good news?*

"Have you thought about what you'll do?" Mr. Ramirez asked Emily.

She nodded. "I want to do something with plants. One book I read mentioned music helps plants grow. I thought I could compare plants raised with music and without to see if one grows better."

"That sounds like it would make a good project," Mr. Ramirez said. Then he turned to Grace. "Have you thought about yours?"

Once again, Emily was prepared and Grace hadn't even started. "Um, no. I mean, not yet." Now she needed to come up with a project that was as good as Emily's—an almost impossible task. Grace sank lower in her chair.

"We have two days to think of ideas," Emily said.

"I'm sure Grace will come up with a good idea by Wednesday."

"You know," Mrs. Ramirez said, "when I was in school, one of my classmates trained a chicken to play a toy piano by putting corn on the keys. That was the coolest science project I'd ever seen. Perhaps, since we have so many animals, you could come up with an animal-related project."

"I guess," Grace mumbled. Getting a chicken to play the piano did sound pretty awesome, but they didn't have any chickens. And they didn't have a piano. Plus, something like that would take a lot of patience.

Patience wasn't one of Grace's strong points. *Mom would tell me to call it a* growth point. *If impatience is a growth point, does that mean I have to work to overcome it?* Grace sighed.

If you called them *faults* or *weaknesses*, you could excuse them. If you called them *growth points*, you had to work on them to grow and change. Her mom had kind of tricked her with that one.

Grace perked up, though, when Abby shared her news.

"I learned a lot about llamas today," Abby told them. "I researched them online and also called Mr. Williams. I want to find out why our llama seems to be avoiding us."

Grace listened intently. Maybe Abby could help

her with this. It really hurt her feelings that Harry turned his back to her every time she fed him or stopped near his enclosure.

"I told Mr. Williams that our llama eyes us as if he might be interested when we talk to him, but as soon as we move closer, he looks down his nose, turns his back, and saunters away. In fact, we mostly only see his tail."

"What did Mr. Williams say about that?" Grace asked.

"He explained that it's best not to look llamas in the eye. Instead, we should wait for them to approach us."

Grace nodded. That's what Emily had done. How had her sister automatically known the right thing to do? Grace let her chile rellenos grow cold on her plate as she leaned forward in her seat to hear everything Abby had learned.

"Mr. Williams said that some behaviors offend llamas. For example, they don't like you to touch their heads or the back of their necks, or to walk right behind them."

Have I done any of those things? Grace tried to remember.

"Because most people were feeding the llama at the petting zoo, the llama came close enough to be touched, and he accepted people petting him while he ate. Often though, he turned his back on visitors."

"That's what he did the last time we saw him in the zoo." Grace forked a bite of dinner into her mouth. Harry had also done that every time since—even when she brought food, he ignored her. He waited until she left to eat.

"Mr. Williams said llamas can feel threatened if you look them in the eye, so you should look at their feet and talk softly as you walk slowly toward them. One internet site said singing can comfort llamas and make them feel more comfortable around you."

"I imagine it depends on who's doing the singing," Mr. Ramirez teased. "I'm not sure my frog-croaking would soothe a llama."

Everyone laughed. Grace wondered what kinds of songs llamas preferred. Maybe she could experiment to find out. Then she sighed so loudly that all eyes turned toward her.

"Are you all right, Grace?" Mrs. Ramirez asked.

"I'm fine. I was trying to think of a science project." The first idea she'd thought of about testing songs for llamas was too much like Emily's music one. Everyone would think she'd copied her sister.

"I'm sure you'll come up with something interesting," Natalie said. "You always have creative ideas."

Yeah, right. She had plenty of creative ideas, but most of those got her into trouble.

Grace listened carefully to the rest of Abby's instructions and planned to try them out after dinner when they did their chores. After shoveling in the rest of her meal, Grace gulped her milk and waited impatiently for everyone else to finish.

The minute dinner was over, she raced out the back door, grateful that doing dishes wasn't one of her chores tonight. Natalie and Abby had dish duty, and Emily was printing out some information for her science project, so Grace went out alone.

Behind her, she heard her parents remark they'd never seen her so eager to do her chores. That was true, but she hadn't hurried to get her chores done. She wanted to see if Abby's ideas worked.

She slowed when she reached the enclosure because she didn't want to startle Harry. He was at the far end of his pen, facing her direction. She was going to step inside, even though her mom had warned her that he might not like it. *How else am I going to make progress with Harry?*

Grace eased the gate open as slowly as she could. Then, without looking at him, she stood near his feedbox.

For several long minutes, nothing happened. Then the llama took a few steps in her direction and hesitated. *Will he come closer?*

Grace held her breath. When she didn't move, he kept coming. She started to hold out her hand. Just in time, she remembered Abby's instructions not to extend her arm and let it drop to her side. This would be the hard part. Abby had said you had to let the llama come to you and sniff you.

Grace tried to stay still as a statue as she waited. And waited . . . And waited . . . Maybe Harry didn't want to be her friend. Every part of Grace's body wanted to wriggle. She almost blew out a breath and gave up.

Then Harry slowly lifted his chin. Grace kept her eyes on his feet and hardly dared to breathe. He headed her way. She could barely stop her excitement from bursting through. She wanted to dance and shout as he came closer, but she forced all her muscles to remain rigid.

Harry came nearer. And nearer. Then he was close enough that she could reach out and touch him. She squeezed her hands into fists to keep them by her side.

Then a miracle happened. Her llama bent his long neck and sniffed her. Grace's heart sang with excitement. She couldn't believe it! Harry was actually sniffing her. She was so thrilled, she couldn't remember what Abby had said to do next.

Something about petting their necks. Was it the front or back? The front was closer, so Grace reached out a tentative hand and stroked the llama's neck.

He didn't back away, so she must have guessed right. She breathed out a long breath, startling Harry. He backed up a few steps, and Grace's heart sank.

"Sorry," she said in her softest voice. "I didn't mean to scare you."

He stayed where he was.

Abby had said llamas liked singing. But what songs did you sing to a llama? The first song that came to mind was the lullaby her birth mother used to sing after she read bedtime stories.

"Listen, Harry," Grace said soothingly. "I don't know what kind of music you like, but I named you after a stuffed animal that reminds me of my mom.

You're my memory llama, so I hope it's okay to sing you my favorite lullaby."

Grace closed her eyes and slipped back to their Dallas apartment. She and Emily had just had baths and were dressed in footie pajamas, each clutching their own special stuffed animal. They snuggled next to Mom, one on each side, while she read. Then, right before she kissed them goodnight, she sang their special bedtime song.

Grace wanted to sing that lullaby to Harry, but the first few words came out choked. Still, Grace kept singing, soft and low, the way her mom had sung to her. The gentle lullaby floated out into the night air. And Grace was back snuggling her mom again. When she finished, her eyes were wet. She opened them to a llama staring at her. The two of them looked at each other for a long time.

When dusk fell, Mr. Ramirez called out, "Grace, are you done with your chores?"

"I have to go," she told the llama. While she'd been with him, her sisters had finished their barn chores, but she hadn't even started. "I have work to do, but I'm glad we've started being friends." She turned to leave but couldn't resist one last peek. "Bye, Harry," she said.

And this time when she looked at him, he met her eyes. *Did his lips curve into a smile?* Grace wasn't sure, but she thought they might have.

Chapter Seven

The next day at school, she asked Ms. Montes if she could do a project with her llama.

After Grace explained what she had in mind, her teacher said, "That sounds interesting, Grace."

Did that mean Ms. Montes approved? "So can I do it?" Grace asked.

Her teacher laughed. "Yes, you may. But you still have to turn in your proposal tomorrow, explaining it."

Grace had been hoping she wouldn't have to do that part, because figuring out how she was going to do her experiment was the hard part. She also had to come up with a hypothesis that she'd prove or disprove.

That night at dinner, she told her family about getting Ms. Montes's approval for her science project.

"That's great, Grace," her mom said. "What did you decide to do?"

"I'm going to train Harry to come when I call."

"That sounds interesting," Natalie said. "When Mom talked about the chicken-and-piano experiment, I looked up information on training animals. That technique is called *operant conditioning.*"

"Would you write that down for me?" Grace asked. If she put big words like that in her proposal, maybe

Ms. Montes would be impressed and give her a better grade. "And can you explain what it is?"

Natalie explained it was a way to train animals—and people—by giving them rewards as they slowly learned to do something new. "It also sometimes uses punishment and other things, but I don't think you'd need that part of it."

"Actually," Emily said, "I think that's what I do with Midnight."

"Exactly," said Natalie. "You've slowly been teaching Midnight to accept a rider. You reward him when he does it right, and then you add another step to move him along to the next level. By not rewarding him with attention when he does things wrong, you're also extinguishing those behaviors."

"Could you write all this down for me, Natalie?" Grace asked.

Natalie shook her head. "If this is for your science project, you should be looking up this information yourself. I'll give you a list of sources I read."

Their mom nodded. "She's right. Why don't you read those articles or books, and then add that information to your report? You can also put those sources in a bibliography."

"If you need help with that, Grace, we're learning the proper formatting for bibliographies in my language arts class," Natalie added. "I can show you what I've learned."

"Thanks, Nat. Ms. Montes didn't say we had to list any sources, but maybe she'd give me extra credit for doing it."

"That would help your science grade," her dad pointed out.

Grace sighed and stared down at her plate. *Why did he have to remind me of that?* Resentment filled her that he had brought it up at the dinner table, where they always tried to have positive conversations. She looked up and mumbled, "I can't help it that I'm not as good in science as Emily is."

"Is that the truth, Grace?" Her dad stared at her until she lowered her eyes again.

"I guess not." She swung her legs under the table, back and forth, back and forth. This wasn't fair. The great llama information Abby had given her had made her happy. She'd started to make friends with Harry. It was like a special secret. A way to get close to her llama. And Natalie had given her an idea for her science project. Then her dad had to spoil it by reminding her of her problems in science class.

Mr. Ramirez cleared his throat. "I know we don't usually talk about negative things during the meal, so I'd like to find a way to turn this into a positive. First of all, I want to point out that you and Emily are both intelligent and capable of getting good grades."

"I know, I know," Grace said. "But Emily spends more time studying, so she gets higher grades." If her parents had said it once, they'd said it a hundred times.

Grace disliked homework and did the bare minimum to get by. She did the same when it came time for tests. Emily read all the study sheets the teacher sent home and often asked their mom to test her. Mom usually asked Grace to join them, but she rarely did. But the times when she listened in to Mom and

Emily practicing the questions and answers, she did much better.

It was so boring, though. And Grace hated to be bored.

She really liked this science project idea. Instead of just sitting in a chair and reading facts, they'd actually get to do something. She also liked the science classes where they did experiments. She wished they did that all the time.

While the others took their turns sharing news, Grace vowed that she'd do a good job on this science project. The best job ever. Maybe she'd manage to make a better grade than Emily and surprise her parents. But first, she had to get Harry to cooperate.

Grace followed Emily into the barn that evening because she had an idea—a creative idea she hoped would make her science project extra special. Her sister was helping Natalie bring the miniature donkeys inside for the night.

Grace trailed her sisters into the barn. "Hey, Emily, I was thinking I could do videos of my llama training to include with my science project."

"That sounds like a fun idea," Natalie said as she tried to calm her kicking donkey.

Evidently, he didn't want to be cooped up inside.

He was used to staying in his enclosure at the zoo all night, but here, they needed to keep the animals safe from predators.

"I'm sorry, Moonbeam," Natalie said. "Why can't you follow Starlight and act like her?"

"Is that what you named them?" Grace asked as she stepped out of the way of the donkey's hooves. They might be tiny, but they delivered a powerful kick.

"Yes, but now I wish I hadn't. Right before dinner, someone emailed about buying them. It's hard to lose animals after you've named them."

Grace swallowed hard. What if someone wanted to adopt Harry? She'd be heartbroken. And what about her science project? "Natalie, should we take Harry off the website while I'm doing my project?"

"That makes sense. I'll do it tonight after chores."

"Thanks." At least Grace had saved Harry for the next few weeks, but then what? And speaking of her science project, she'd come out to the barn to talk to her sister about video recording her and Harry.

"So, Emily, do you think you could video me now before it gets too dark? I want one picture where Harry's avoiding me."

Her sister didn't answer as she led Moonbeam into a stall and then helped Natalie settle Starlight. When she did answer, all the air and anticipation leaked out of Grace.

"I'd like to help you, but I haven't even started on my chores. Plus, I have a lot of homework. Actually, you do too. And I need to set up my plant experiment."

Grace was disappointed Emily wasn't willing to help her. "But how can I get the videos?"

"I'll try to help you, but just not tonight. I want to recheck my science project proposal."

"Oh." Grace had forgotten that was due tomorrow. She'd have to do hers too. "If I helped you by taking care of some of your animals, would you have time then?"

"I guess so. What animals did you plan to help me with?"

"I can scatter the food down by the pond and feed the other birds. Would that be enough? The video doesn't have to be long."

"Okay," Emily said. "I'll take care of the hedgehog and the skunk, and then meet you at Harry's pen."

Grace hurried to get the birds fed so she'd be back in time to meet Emily. So far, none of the birds had flown away; they must have decided to stay for the food. Their mom had mentioned possibly retraining them so they could live in the wild, although she said she didn't know if it were possible.

Emily was just heading outside as Grace jogged back from the pond. She pulled out her cell phone and handed it to Emily.

Then she opened the gate. She hoped Harry would

do his usual ignoring-her routine, at least until Emily shot the video. "If you just take a short clip of me going through the gate and Harry keeping his back to me, that'd be good."

Grace tried not to startle Harry or do any of the things Abby had warned against. She hoped he'd come to her again tonight, but not before they got the videos.

"Okay," Emily said, "I'm going to turn on the video."

Grace waved to the camera and then turned her back and entered the enclosure. Harry remained turned away from her. Grace talked softly, but the llama didn't respond.

"It's off now!" Emily called.

"Thanks," Grace said, hoping Emily hadn't startled Harry. "Could you take it into the house when you go? I'm going to see if I can connect with Harry."

Evidently picking up her clues from Grace's quieter voice, Emily lowered hers. "Do you want me to film you trying?"

"Sure." She could use the new video as a second step in the process. It would be great to have two videos done already before the project even officially started. What would her parents say when they found out she'd completed part of her project already? Although, she still had a long way to go. And what would happen if she couldn't get Harry to cooperate?

Maybe Emily would use her animal-whispering skills to help.

Grace repeated all the steps from the night before, and slowly, Harry responded.

As Harry came near and let Grace pet him, Emily sucked in a breath. She flicked off the camera. "I'm not recording anymore," she said in a hoarse whisper.

But Emily stayed leaning on the gate while Grace sang the lullaby, and she quietly joined in after the second line.

Grace wanted to hug Harry after it was over, but she resisted the urge. *Am I already learning to be a little more patient*? She could tell her mom she'd grown some.

As she exited the enclosure and locked the gate behind her, Emily handed over the cell phone. "That was beautiful," her sister said with tears in her eyes. "I'm so happy we got Harry. He's bringing back special memories."

"I know. I wish we could keep him forever." Grace turned to Emily. "Thank you for taking the video."

"You're welcome. You should take those videos off the phone to make room for more. Maybe Dad would let you take his laptop to school to use for your science project. If so, you can put the videos on there or in the cloud. Just so you can get them when you need them."

"That's a great idea," Grace said. She'd have the best science project ever.

For once, she was eager to do her homework, so she hurried through the rest of her chores. By the time she got back up to the bedroom she shared with her twin, Emily was already seated at her desk, scribbling away.

Grace washed up and sat down at her desk. She dug through her backpack and pulled out the crumpled sheet her teacher had given her. After a hunt through the mess in her desk drawer, she found a pencil and filled in the blanks on her proposal worksheet:

Hypothesis:

A llama can be trained to come when he's called.

Procedure (Steps for Proving Hypothesis):

1) Plan the best time of day for training.

2) Figure out rewards that llamas love.

3) Decide what behaviors get rewards.

4) Give the llama rewards every time he does what he's supposed to do.

5) Repeat until the llama can do the task with only one reward at the end.

Predicted Result:

Llama will come when called.

When she finished, she printed her name neatly at the top of the paper and shoved the paper back into her bag.

"I'm done with my sheet," Grace announced. "Are you?"

Emily's head was bent low over the desk, and she was gnawing on a pencil. "No, I'm still not sure my steps are detailed enough."

Grace had pondered over her list, but Ms. Montes would correct them. She'd fix anything Grace had missed.

🐾

On Thursday, Ms. Montes handed back the proposals, and Grace peeked at Emily's. Hers had "Excellent job!" at the top and no comments. Then Grace got hers, with red pen scribbled everywhere. It did say, "Interesting idea," but the comments scattered throughout said things like, "What distance will the llama travel? Be specific." Also, "Check the difference between classical and operant conditioning." A few comments offered additional steps for her procedure section.

Grace slumped in her seat. She thought she'd done

a good job, but once again, Emily had done better. *It just isn't fair. Why does Emily always sail through easily, while I get stuck with check marks, comments, and lower grades?*

She grew even more discouraged when Ms. Montes explained about the proposals.

"Some of you may have received some comments on your papers," Ms. Montes said. "If you did, I'd like you to rework them and resubmit them by Monday. I want to be sure everyone has a good framework to begin their project."

Grace plunked her elbows on her desk and put her head in her hands. Not only had Emily gotten hers right the first time, she wouldn't have any science homework over the weekend. Doubly unfair!

Chapter Eight

That night at dinner, Emily shared about her project getting approved, and how she'd already set up her experiment. She'd put the plants in their bedroom with classical music, which made Grace grit her teeth when she was in the bedroom, because she didn't like "old people music." The other plants had been placed in their parents' bedroom, where it was quiet.

Mrs. Ramirez turned to Grace with a huge smile. "How did your teacher like your project?" From the excited expression in her eyes, her mom was expecting another big hit.

Grace gulped. She didn't want to tell them about all the mistakes and red comments, so she lifted her chin. "She said it was interesting." That at least was true. She hoped it would be enough to deflect other questions.

"Great." Now her dad was also beaming at her.

No pressure or anything. Somehow, she had to make this the best science project ever. But she had no idea how to do that.

After she'd finished the dinner dishes and her chores, she went into the family room, where Natalie was typing a report for school.

"Hey, Nat, could you—?"

Her sister held up a finger to stop Grace from talking. Grace stood there waiting while Natalie typed furiously. After what seemed like an eternity, her sister looked up. "Sorry, but if I didn't get that written, I'd forget it. What did you want?"

It had taken so long, Grace had almost forgotten her question. "Would you help me set up my science project?" she asked.

"Have you read those websites I gave you?"

Grace shuffled her feet on the floor. "Not yet, but I will."

Natalie fixed her with a stern expression. "Look, Grace. I'm willing to help, but only if you do your own work. It's not fair to ask me to do your homework."

"I didn't mean for you to do my homework," Grace said defensively.

"Then come back and see me after you've read the material, and we can talk."

"I can't look up anything when you're using the computer," Grace pointed out.

Natalie shook her head. "No excuses. You have a phone. Read it on there."

"Oh, okay." Grace hadn't thought of that.

Natalie softened a little. "I'll send you a link to information about Pavlov."

"Huh?" Grace felt like she was getting in over her head. She wanted to do the hands-on training, not read a bunch of theories.

"He did some interesting work with dogs," Natalie explained.

I am working with a llama, not a dog. But whatever. Grace sighed and sank onto the family room couch and pulled up the sites on her phone. Most of them were difficult to slog through. She wasn't sure she understood much about how animal training worked, but she'd watched Emily train Midnight. Her sister did one small action, then when Midnight did it well, she rewarded him.

The information about Pavlov was more interesting than she expected. He had discovered that he could make dogs *salivate*—she looked up that word to find out it meant the way your mouth filled with spit when you were hungry or thought about food. By ringing a bell every time he brought the dogs food, the dogs began to salivate whenever they heard the bell, even if he didn't bring food.

Grace leaned her head back against the couch and closed her eyes, trying to picture the hungry dogs with their dripping mouths. She didn't want to make Harry salivate, so why had Natalie suggested she read this article?

All of a sudden, she leaped up. "I've got it."

Natalie jumped and clutched her hands to her chest. "Sheesh, Grace, you scared me. And look at that." She pointed to the computer screen.

Her hand must have hit the computer keys,

because she'd typed a few letters of gibberish. She highlighted and deleted them.

"Sorry," Grace said, "but I got this great idea. You know that Pavlov guy? Well, I didn't want to make Harry salivate, but I realized Pavlov paired two things: the bell and dinner. What if I teach Harry to come with a song instead of a bell?"

"Didn't Abby tell us llamas liked songs?" Natalie

asked. When Grace nodded, Natalie smiled at her. "That's brilliant!"

Grace beamed. So maybe she'd have a great science project after all.

Natalie closed out her document. "Why don't we get you started on your project, and then I can work on my paper with fewer interruptions."

Was Natalie implying Grace was a bother? She shriveled a little inside, but then she reminded herself that Natalie had called her idea *brilliant*. And her sister had agreed to help her. Grace pushed aside her hurt thoughts and concentrated on the present moment. "So what do we do first?"

"Why don't you describe what you're thinking of doing and the steps you've thought of so far?"

So Grace listed her procedure, and Natalie made suggestions. Like Ms. Montes had suggested, Natalie helped her establish ways to measure Harry's progress. Then Grace looked up llama treats online. It seemed llamas liked carrots, apples, and peppermints, the way the horses on the ranch did, but one site also suggested broccoli, watermelon, and sweet potatoes. The websites suggested slicing up fruits and vegetables into small bites.

When she and Natalie were done, Grace wanted to race outside and get started, but she'd have to wait until tomorrow.

She did rewrite her proposal using the ideas she

and Natalie had developed, and she turned it in the next day, even though it wasn't due until Monday. Ms. Montes handed it back after lunch with one comment at the top of the page: "Interesting and creative project!"

Was that better than Emily's "Excellent job!" remark? Ms. Montes had used two adjectives on hers and only one on Emily's. But was "Interesting and creative" as good as "Excellent"? Somehow, it didn't seem like it was. Her parents would tell her that she needed to stop comparing herself to Emily and just do her best. Grace tried to tell herself that was true, but it didn't help. She still wanted to do as well as her twin.

The rest of the day, Grace struggled to pay attention because she was busy daydreaming about training Harry. Ms. Montes would probably be surprised to know how excited Grace was about doing her science project.

As soon as she got home from school, Grace checked their fruit and vegetable bins for treats. She found a few sweet potatoes, so she sliced up one and put it into a plastic bag so Harry couldn't smell the pieces. Then she hurried out to his pen.

She repeated the waiting she'd done the other times, and when Harry reached her, she slid one bite of sweet potato onto the palm of her hand and slowly extended it. Harry snuffled her hand and then closed his lips around the treat.

While he was eating, Grace sang snatches of the lullaby. She stopped when he finished chewing. Then she stepped a few feet away, took out another bite, and set it on her hand. As soon as Harry touched her hand with his lips, she sang quietly so she wouldn't startle him.

She spent about an hour repeating the routine before realizing she should have been recording her actions. "Just a minute, Harry. I'll be right back."

Grace raced into the house and upstairs. She burst into the bedroom. "Emily, can you come quickly and record me?"

Her sister had been painting a watercolor that looked like a hedgehog, but now the paper had a huge slash of brown paint right through the middle of it. Emily turned and stared at Grace with sad eyes.

Emily had always begged Grace to enter the room quietly, but often Grace got so excited, she forgot. Like today. "I'm sorry," she said.

"This one was going really well. I'd just figured out how to paint the spines so they looked right." Emily closed her eyes and looked as if she were about to cry.

Grace wished she could go back and redo the last few minutes. Would she ever learn to stop and think before acting? "I'm sorry," she said again, but the words couldn't erase the damage she'd done.

Emily's eyes flickered open, and she stared at Grace with a look that broke Grace's heart. "I spent more than an hour working on this. Now I have to start all over again."

"I know." Grace hung her head. "I should have come in quietly."

"Also," Emily continued, "I'm doing my science experiment in here, so I wanted the plants to only hear gentle noises and music." She plunked both her elbows onto the desk and rested her chin in her hands. "I wish I could put the plants somewhere else, but our windowsill is the only one that exactly matches Mom and Dad's. They face the same way, get the same amount of sunlight, and they're far enough apart that the music doesn't penetrate their walls."

"Oh." Grace hadn't meant to ruin her sister's project. "I promise I'll be more careful next time."

"You know, Grace, you make that same promise every few days, but a day or two later, you forget."

Emily was right. Grace needed to do something to remind herself to keep her promise. "I have an idea. Why don't we make a sign and post it on our bedroom door? Maybe if I see that, I'll stop and remember to enter quietly."

"Guess it can't hurt," Emily said. "I suppose you want me to make it?"

"Would you?" Grace said. "You're so good at it."

Emily thought for a minute, then she brushed

her hand over her paper. "This is dry," she said. After flipping the paper over, she painted a small plant in the lower corner of the paper. Then, with bright-red paint, she added large capitalized words: "SLOW DOWN." Under that, she put the word "NOISE" in a large red circle with a slash through it.

"Well, that's bright enough that I'll see it before I barge into the room," Grace said. "While that's drying, will you come outside and take a video of me with Harry?"

"I suppose so. It'll soon be dinnertime, so I don't have enough time to start another painting." She gestured toward the warning sign on her desk and sighed. "I guess this will have to be my painting project for today."

"Thanks, Em, and I'm really, really sorry." Grace picked up her phone. "I'll try to be more careful and read the sign." She motioned for Emily to follow her. "Wait until you see what Harry can do."

Although she was bursting to tell Emily, she decided to surprise her sister instead. When she reached the pen, she said, "Get ready to video something awesome."

Grace entered the gate, while Emily propped her elbows on the top of the gate to keep the camera steady. Grace went to the spot where she'd been successful earlier. Harry had his back to her.

"Should I start the video now?" Emily asked.

"Let's wait till Harry starts turning around," Grace suggested.

So they waited. Minutes ticked by. Nothing happened. Harry stayed in one place and didn't head toward Grace. She tried singing, calling his name, holding out a piece of sweet potato. Because he'd seemed friendly earlier, she walked up behind him and petted the back of his head.

"Oh, Grace, no!" Emily called. "Remember what Abby said?"

Harry's mouth was moving like he was chewing. He turned toward her but flattened back his ears and squinted a bit. Then he made a strange gurgling noise, and liquid shot out of his mouth straight at Grace. She jumped away from the stream. The stinky mess barely missed her shoes, and instead splatted on the ground.

"Ugh! That smells horrible!" Emily exclaimed.

"Ugh! That's disgusting!" Grace quickly stepped out of the pen and closed the gate behind her. "And he was doing so well just a little bit ago. I promise."

I hope I haven't made a big mistake taking on this science project.

🐾

That night at dinner, Grace told about her success with Harry after school, but she also told about him spitting at her.

"Maybe he didn't like Emily being there," Natalie suggested. "Or perhaps he was letting you know he was tired of the game."

"But Emily videoed him before, and he didn't seem to mind."

"You know," Abby said, "llamas don't like you to follow them or touch the backs of their necks. Maybe you startled him by coming up from behind. Or maybe he's accepted you as another llama and is acting like he would around the herd. But watch his ears. When he pins them back, look out."

"I did notice that, and I managed to jump out of the way."

"You're lucky." Abby leaned forward and asked, "Was it like a spray mist or a rancid green fluid?"

Grace's whole face wrinkled up as she recalled the goo. "It was stinky and greenish."

Abby glanced at their mom. "I know Mom doesn't like this kind of talk at the table, but llamas have three stomach compartments, and because their spit is really vomit, it sounds like it came from the third stomach. Did it smell rotten and icky?"

Grace nodded. "It stunk like crazy. Like vinegar and rotting food."

"That makes sense," Abby said, "because the vomit is from the food they're digesting and—"

When Mom frowned, Abby stopped talking about vomiting, but she added one more comment. "Did you know llama vom— . . . er . . . spit can go ten to fifteen feet?"

"Yikes!" Grace was glad she'd leaped out of the way, but maybe she needed to keep an eye on Harry's ears. She didn't want to get showered with any goop.

Grace knew she should pay attention to the rest of the family's sharing, but she retreated into her own thoughts. She had to find a way to get Harry to cooperate. Now, at least, she knew not to sneak up on him from behind.

Chapter Nine

For the next week, Grace made sure to let Harry come to her, rather than chasing after him. It took a lot of willpower for her to stand still and wait for him to approach. It was worth it, though, because Harry cooperated with the training, and Emily got some good videos.

Grace also did her best to slow down and read the sign Emily had posted on the door. Emily made several good hedgehog paintings and even gave Grace one as a thank you for coming into the room quietly for several days in a row. But all this being patient and thinking ahead was hard work, for sure.

One day before dinner as she hurried through her chores, Natalie stopped her. "I know you're eager to work with Harry, but some of your other animals need attention."

"No, they don't," Grace protested. "I fed and watered all of them."

"That's a good start," Natalie said, "but animals also need some time, attention, and affection." She pointed to the pig. "Look at Daisy. She's trying to tell you she wants your company. Why don't you play with her for a little while?"

Grace turned toward the huge pig, who was

grunting. *Ugh!* Daisy was huge and kind of scary. "What am I supposed to do with her?"

"Maybe you could talk to her, scratch her back, feed her a treat."

"Um, all right." Talking to Daisy wouldn't be so bad. She wouldn't have to get close to her. And at least she didn't have to worry about Daisy spitting at her.

🐾

On Saturday morning, Grace juggled her soccer ball into the barn to do her morning chores. She had to leave for her game in an hour, so she wanted to limber up and work on ball control. The ball arced from knee to knee. *Tap. Tap. Tap.* Quick header. Back to knee. *Bounce. Bounce.* Side of foot. *Tap-tap.* She'd just gotten into the rhythm when she reached Daisy's pen. Seeing the pig made her nervous, and she bounced the ball off her knee too hard. It sailed over the railing and landed right in front of Daisy.

How can I get it back? I'm not going in there.

The pig snuffled the soccer ball. Then she pushed it with her nose.

"Keep coming, Daisy," Grace begged. "I'll give you a treat." She reached in her pocket for a slice of sweet potato she'd planned to give Harry.

Daisy lifted her head and sniffed. Grace shook her head and hid the sweet potato.

"No, you have to push the ball over here first. Then you can have the treat."

The pig seemed to understand and returned to pushing the ball with her nose.

Grace squatted down. "That's it, Daisy. You can do it."

When the pig got closer, Grace held out the treat. Again, Daisy lifted her head and seemed about to come for the treat, but Grace hid it until Daisy pushed the ball in her direction. Soon, the ball was near enough to grab. But Grace didn't want to reach into the pen. She tossed the sweet potato a short distance behind the pig. While Daisy went after it, Grace snatched up her ball.

Abby passed by. "Are you teaching Daisy to play ball with you? That might be easier than training a llama. Pigs learn fast."

Grace sighed. Too bad she'd already submitted her science project idea. The thought of playing ball with Daisy made her nervous, so maybe she was better off with Harry. Except for the spitting. She only hoped she could get him to cooperate before her project was due.

Later that afternoon, Grace headed to the garage for the pump for her soccer ball. Her ball had lost some air, so she wanted to fill it. As Grace jumped to reach the pump on a tall shelf, a bunch of sports equipment—Frisbees, gloves, and balls—rained down around her. She dug through the mess to find her pump, then kicked everything else to the side as a way of cleaning it up. When she did so, a small blue ball rolled from the pile and bounced across the garage floor.

It gave Grace an idea. Maybe she could throw the ball in Daisy's pen to keep the pig occupied. After she pumped up the ball, she went inside to cut up an apple. Then, on her way to see Harry, she detoured past the pig's enclosure to drop off the ball.

"Here, Daisy," she said as she tossed the ball into the pen.

Daisy's deep oinking made Grace nervous, and she stepped farther away. But when the pig used her snout to roll the ball toward Grace, she stopped to watch. Daisy pushed the ball under the lowest wooden rail. The floor sloped, so the ball ended up at Grace's feet. She kicked it back into the pen, and Daisy returned it. Grace laughed. The pig really did want to play. She tossed Daisy the ball and an apple slice.

While Daisy went after them, Grace slipped away to work with Harry. But her mind was on Daisy. Maybe she could teach Daisy to bowl. If she got some empty plastic water bottles, could Daisy knock them over?

Today, without Emily watching, Harry behaved. If only she could get Emily out here to capture their session. She had to find a way to document Harry's progress.

"Grace," Emily called from the house, "it's our turn to make dinner."

With a sigh, Grace handed Harry one last piece of apple. "I have to go, but you were a good boy today." Then she trudged to the house. As much as Grace liked eating, she didn't always enjoy cooking. She made too many mistakes. Emily did a much better job at following recipes.

Grace went into the kitchen and washed up. Yesterday, they'd decided on migas for dinner, and Emily had already gotten out the eggs, milk, and cheese. Sometimes, they had them for breakfast, but it was an easy dinner to make. Emily had placed two frying pans on the stove and had placed a layer of corn chips on each plate.

"I'll let you make the spicy scrambled eggs," she said. "I'll make plain ones for Abby and me. Do you want to call everyone?"

"Sure." Grace yelled for the family to come for dinner. Migas cooked fast, so everyone needed to be at the table and ready to eat if they wanted their meal hot.

They both heated oil, and Grace added chopped onions and jalapeño peppers, then stirred them around to soften them, while Emily mixed the eggs and milk. She poured some of the mixture into her pan and handed the rest to Grace. Before Grace poured it in, she stirred in salsa. Then she mixed it with the onions and jalapeños to make it nice and spicy, just the way she liked it. She couldn't understand how Abby and Emily could stand such bland food.

When the eggs were almost set, she and Emily both dumped in grated cheese and stirred it around to melt it. They quickly scooped portions onto the corn chips and served the meals. Emily had set a lazy Susan in the center of the table filled with pico de gallo, cheese, sour cream, salsa, avocado, cilantro, and beans. While Emily and Abby added a little salt to their migas, the rest of the family piled on more spices and toppings.

"Good job, girls," their mom said after she'd chewed a few bites.

For once, Grace hadn't spilled, dropped, or burned anything. She wondered if their mom was complimenting her on a disaster-free day or letting them know she liked the food.

Because her mouth was full, Grace mumbled, "Thanks." Once she finished chewing, she told about Daisy and the ball, and about how well Harry was doing. "I just wish Emily could get pictures," she added. "Every time Emily shows up, Harry refuses to cooperate."

"Maybe if Emily came to watch a few sessions," Abby suggested, "Harry would get used to her being there."

"We'll have to try that." Grace hoped it would work. She really wanted to have the video to prove what she'd done. "Can you come out after dinner?" she asked Emily.

"I guess so. I still have homework to do. Don't you? Unless you already studied for the science test?"

Grace groaned. She'd forgotten about it, but now that Emily had mentioned it in front of their parents, she'd have to study.

Once the meal was over, she and Emily headed for Harry's pen. Grace handed over her cell phone, just in case Harry performed in front of Emily. She stood and waited for Harry to come to her. Next, she stepped a few feet away and held out a piece of carrot, hoping Harry would walk over to eat it. And he did! Grace hoped Emily had caught that on video. She sang the lullaby while Harry ate.

Then she moved farther away. Again, he came to her. After a few more tries, she increased the gap between them. When Harry finally wandered off, Grace rushed over to Emily.

"Did you get it?" she asked, bouncing up and down. "That's the first time he's come that far."

Smiling, Emily handed back Grace's phone. "I think I got it all. You were right, it was awesome." She turned to head toward the barn. "Now we need to finish our chores, so we have plenty of time to study."

Grace bit back a moan. *Why do I have to ruin a great day with studying?* She took care of her animals and spent a little time playing with Daisy. Maybe she could use some empty water bottles next weekend to experiment with bowling.

After her chores, she slogged back to the room where her mom was testing Emily on questions from the study sheet Ms. Montes had given them. Grace knew the answers to a few questions, but most of the time, she just listened to Emily's answers.

When she took the test the next day, Grace was surprised at how easy it was. She remembered most of the questions from the night before. If she hadn't studied, she might have missed a lot more questions. And several days later, when she got her test back with an A at the top, she was glad she'd studied. Maybe Mom was right that she could get grades as good as Emily. Grace knew one thing for sure: Her science project was going to be one of the best ever.

She worked with Harry every day, and he cooperated well and allowed Emily to take a few more videos. Grace kept forgetting to transfer them to her dad's laptop, but she still had enough memory on her phone for all the ones they'd taken. The afternoon before their science project was due, Grace asked Emily to take the final video.

Harry was across the field when she entered his enclosure. Grace stepped inside and sang the lullaby. Usually, he sauntered over slowly, but this time, he practically galloped toward her. Grace rewarded him with extra treats.

"Did you get a video of that?" she asked Emily.

Her sister nodded. "It was awesome. I think Ms. Montes is going to love your project."

"Thanks," Grace said. She couldn't wait to see her teacher's face when she saw the videos.

She thanked Harry and practically skipped to the barn to do her chores.

She'd also spent a little time with Daisy every day. After collecting six empty water bottles, she'd arranged them like bowling pins. Although she still felt nervous around the huge pig, she'd go into the pen and set up the plastic bottles. Then she'd roll the ball to Daisy, who'd shove it with her nose. The slight slope of the ground helped to keep the ball rolling until it knocked over some pins.

Today, Grace, thrilled about finishing her Harry project on time, played the bowling game four times with Daisy. On her last try, Daisy knocked over all six pins. Grace cheered for her and even scratched her back.

Grace went into the house for dinner with a bounce in her step and bounded up the stairs to tell Emily. She almost banged into the bedroom, but the poster on the door stopped her. It took a lot of will-power, but she forced herself to turn the doorknob quietly.

After she stepped into the room, she was glad she hadn't burst through the door and startled Emily, because her sister was painting small pictures on her science poster board. Grace waited until Emily lifted her paintbrush from the board and dipped it in the paint before she spoke.

"Hey, Em, that looks good."

Emily looked up. "Oh, Grace. I didn't hear you come in."

"That's good, right? I wanted to rush in here to

tell you something, but I slowed down because of the poster."

"Great," Emily said. "I'm so glad you did. If you'd made me jump while I was painting, I could have ruined my whole display. Thank you."

The smile her sister gave her made Grace all warm and fuzzy inside. Sometimes, doing hard things was worth it. And that reminded her of Daisy and why she'd run up to the bedroom. She told Emily about the pig and bowling.

"Wow! That's so cool," Emily said. "I'd like to see that." She accompanied Grace to the barn.

One good thing about Daisy was that she wasn't shy. She loved performing in front of Emily, and she grunted happily at the praise, back-scratching, and treats that followed.

🐾

Grace and Emily went in for dinner together, and Grace wriggled until sharing time. When she told everyone she'd finished her science project, they all congratulated her. She invited everyone in the family to go out to the pen after dinner to see Harry come when she sang.

Unfortunately, by the time everyone gathered outside Harry's pen that evening, the llama didn't cooperate. Maybe having all those people staring at him made him as nervous as Grace felt around the pig.

"Never mind," she said. "I have a video of it right here." She passed around her phone so everyone could see.

"Quite an impressive project," her dad said, handing back the phone. "I'm sure your teacher will be thrilled at how much work you put into it." Then he ruffled Emily's hair too. "Yours is wonderful, as well. I'm so proud of both of you."

Emily ducked her head and blushed, but she had a smile on her face that revealed how happy she was. Grace was glad she didn't have to compete with Emily for the best project, because they both had awesome projects. She couldn't wait to take hers to school tomorrow.

Chapter Ten

Grace barely slept that night because she was so excited, and she jumped out of bed the next morning before Emily was awake. She put on her favorite outfit and rechecked the huge poster board she'd prepared that showed her hypothesis, all the steps she'd followed, and her conclusion. Emily's poster board stood on her desk, decorated with paintings and snapshots of the plants as they grew. Emily's project also had bar graphs and a notebook with daily measurements.

Shaking her sister awake, Grace said, "I want to take one more video of me in Harry's pen with my poster board. I'll sing to get him to come over and stand beside me while I hold up the poster board. Wouldn't that be awesome?"

Emily groaned. Usually, she was the first one up, but they'd both stayed up late putting the finishing touches on their displays.

"Come on, Em. Please?"

Her sister rolled out of bed and dressed. Then Grace gave her the phone and picked up her poster board, and they headed out to the pen.

"Sorry I got you up so early," Grace told her, "but I wanted to make one last video, and I need to transfer the videos to Dad's laptop. I'm going to do that before breakfast."

"If you'd done it as you went along, you'd only have to do one this morning," Emily pointed out.

"Yeah, I know, but . . ." Somehow, being around her sister always made Grace feel so inadequate. Maybe it was because Emily always reminded Grace of her growth points. To make herself feel better, Grace reminded herself of all the ways she'd already grown. She'd been super patient in training Harry, and she'd even taught Daisy to bowl. She'd remembered not to barge into the bedroom and disturb Emily. She'd studied for her science test and gotten an A. Thinking about those things made her feel better.

Grace went into Harry's pen carrying her poster board and sang the lullaby. The llama galloped in her direction. Grace's heart overflowed with happiness. The sun was shining, she had on her favorite outfit, Harry was cooperating, and her poster board looked terrific. She'd get this one last video to make it the best morning ever.

Harry stopped right beside her, and Grace held up her poster board. This video would be perfect. Thrilled, she threw her arm around the llama's neck.

Startled, Harry pinned back his ears. Grace had been smiling for the camera, but then came that gurgling sound. The last time Harry had made that noise . . .

As Grace jumped toward the fence near Emily, her huge poster board tripped her up. Disgusting, sticky goop showered over both the girls. And the stink—a smell that was the combination of sauerkraut and skunk spray—made Grace gag.

Her poster board was ruined. And Emily held out the slimed phone.

"That was disgusting!" Grace cried out. "And now my whole project is ruined!" Her videos were ruined! Grace had been counting on an A. Now, the only thing she'd get would be a zero.

The two of them raced to the house. By the time they'd both showered and changed and soaked their clothes so they wouldn't be stained, they had no time for breakfast. They grabbed bananas and granola bars to eat on the way. Abby had already left on the school bus, but their dad had offered to drive them to school so they wouldn't have to lug Emily's plants and poster board on the bus.

While Emily loaded her science project into the back of the SUV, Grace stood, shaking her phone. She had cleaned the llama vomit off of it, but it was no use. No matter how many times she pushed the button, the screen stayed blank. Her dad suggested putting it in a bag of rice to dry it out. Grace followed his advice, but the phone would never dry out in time for school today. And she had no guarantee it would ever work again.

If she'd transferred the videos to her dad's laptop along the way, as Emily had suggested, she'd at least have more to show for her project. But now her poster board was covered in bile, and her videos were gone. With her mom's advice to plan ahead running through her head, Grace climbed into the car. She'd tried getting out of going to school because she felt so sick to her stomach, but both of her parents insisted she had to go anyway.

The closer they got to school, the sicker Grace felt. How could she go into the classroom filled with projects and sit there while everyone explained what they'd done?

When their dad pulled in front of the school, Grace carried Emily's poster board and trailed her sister into school. She set the board on her sister's desk and then trudged to her own desk and plopped down, her eyes burning with unshed tears. Ms. Montes looked at her in surprise.

"Where's your project, Grace?" her teacher asked.

Her voice thick with anguish, Grace said, "A llama spit on my homework."

Ms. Montes's eyes widened, and she shook her head. "Now I've heard everything."

Grace endured sitting through each presentation, and the day seemed to last forever. At least it was Friday, so she wouldn't have to face everyone again until Monday. By then, maybe most people would have forgotten.

Ms. Montes agreed Grace could redo her poster board and take a new video to turn in Monday, but she said, "I know this was an accident, but I'm sure you understand I have to dock your grade for not having your project in on time." She pointed to the rubric on the board, where it clearly said late projects would be dropped one grade lower.

The lump choking Grace's throat prevented her from answering. She could only nod. She understood, but she didn't think it was fair.

and Harry trotted over. The oohs and aahs from her classmates helped make up for her sadness about her grade.

When they went inside to see the barn animals, Mrs. Ramirez suggested that Grace should demonstrate what Daisy could do. So Grace set up the water bottle bowling pins and rolled the ball to Daisy. After Daisy knocked down five of the pins, everyone clapped. Grace's spirits rose, and she almost forgot about her messed-up science project.

"Did your pig know how to do that when you got her?" Zander asked.

Grace shook her head. "No, I taught her. I came up with the idea when I was working with Harry. I tried the same thing with Daisy, and it worked."

"That's so cool," Zander said. "I wish I had an animal I could train. You're so lucky."

By the time they went out to the meadow for lunch, Grace was nearly back to her usual bouncy self. As her classmates sat on the blankets her mom had spread out, Ms. Montes beckoned to Grace.

"Did I understand that you trained your pig at the same time as you trained your llama?" Ms. Montes asked.

Grace nodded.

"Well, I must say, I'm quite impressed with what you've done. You know, ever since I saw that pig bowl,

I've been thinking. I believe you should get extra credit for doing two science projects."

"Really?" Grace's heart raced. Was it possible she might get an A?

"Yes, really." Ms. Montes smiled. "Not everyone would apply what they were learning like that. A lot of time in school, we have students memorize facts, but it's more important to understand how to use them. And you've done that. It's a big accomplishment, Grace, and a gift you have."

Praise from Ms. Montes was worth more to Grace than a higher grade. And hearing that she had "a gift" made her feel better about preferring to learn things hands-on. But her teacher wasn't finished yet.

"I'll be changing your science project grade to reflect your extra credit." Ms. Montes laid a hand on Grace's shoulder. "I think you deserve an A+."

An A+? Grace couldn't believe it. Not just an A, but an A+. "Thank you, Ms. Montes!" Then Grace danced over to join her classmates with a joy-filled heart.

About the Author

When she was young, Laurie J. Edwards brought home many stray dogs and cats. She told her mother they just followed her home, but pieces of leftover meat from her lunch also might have helped to attract them. The pet she wanted most, though, was a horse. Her parents insisted their yard was too small. When she turned thirteen, Laurie began taking riding lessons and spent as much time as she could around horses.

She grew up and became a librarian because she loved books as much as she loved animals. Then she discovered the joys of writing books, as well as reading them. Now she is the author of more than forty books.

About the Illustrator

Jomike Tejido is an author and illustrator who has illustrated the books *I Funny: School of Laughs* and *Middle School: Dog's Best Friend*, as well as the Pet Charms and I Want to Be . . . Dinosaurs! series. He has fond memories of horseback riding as a kid and has always liked drawing fluffy animals. Jomike lives in Manila with his wife, two daughters, and a chow chow named Oso.

Join Natalie, Abby, Emily, and Grace and
read more animal stories in . . .

BY KELSEY ABRAMS

ILLUSTRATED BY JOMIKE TEJIDO

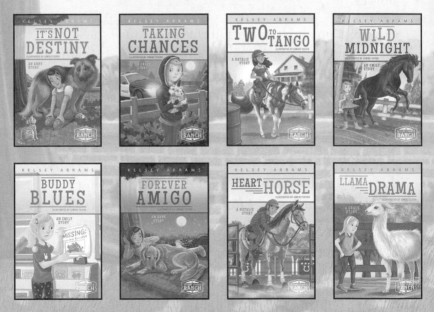

CHARMING MIDDLE GRADE FICTION
FROM JOLLY FISH PRESS